Dear Parent:

Congratulations! Your child is taking the first steps on an exciting journey. The destination? Independent reading!

STEP INTO READING® will help your child get there. The program offers five steps to reading success. Each step includes fun stories and colorful art. There are also Step into Reading Sticker Books, Step into Reading Math Readers, Step into Reading Write-In Readers, Step into Reading Phonics Readers, and Step into Reading Phonics First Steps! Boxed Sets—a complete literacy program with something for every child.

Learning to Read, Step by Step!

Ready to Read Preschool–Kindergarten
• big type and easy words • rhyme and rhythm • picture clues
For children who know the alphabet and are eager to begin reading.

Reading with Help Preschool–Grade 1
• basic vocabulary • short sentences • simple stories
For children who recognize familiar words and sound out new words with help.

Reading on Your Own Grades 1–3
• engaging characters • easy-to-follow plots • popular topics
For children who are ready to read on their own.

Reading Paragraphs Grades 2–3
• challenging vocabulary • short paragraphs • exciting stories
For newly independent readers who read simple sentences with confidence.

Ready for Chapters Grades 2–4
• chapters • longer paragraphs • full-color art
For children who want to take the plunge into chapter books but still like colorful pictures.

STEP INTO READING® is designed to give every child a successful reading experience. The grade levels are only guides. Children can progress through the steps at their own speed, developing confidence in their reading, no matter what their grade.

Remember, a lifetime love of reading starts with a single step!

Text copyright © 1991 by Random House, Inc. Illustrations copyright © 1991 by Darcy May. All rights reserved under International and Pan-American Copyright Conventions. Published in the United States by Random House Children's Books, a division of Random House, Inc., New York, and simultaneously in Canada by Random House of Canada Limited, Toronto.

www.stepintoreading.com

Educators and librarians, for a variety of teaching tools, visit us at www.randomhouse.com/teachers

Library of Congress Cataloging-in-Publication Data
Hautzig, Deborah.
Hans Christian Andersen's The little mermaid / retold by Deborah Hautzig ; illustrated by Darcy May.
   p.   cm. — (Step into reading. A step 4 book)
SUMMARY: A little sea princess, longing to be human, trades her mermaid's tail for legs, hoping to win the love of a prince and earn an immortal soul for herself.
ISBN 0-679-82241-0 (trade) — ISBN 0-679-92241-5 (lib. bdg.)
[1. Fairy tales.   2. Mermaids—Fiction.]   I. Title: Little mermaid.   II. May, Darcy, ill.
III. Andersen, H. C. (Hans Christian), 1805–1875. Lille havfrue. English.   IV. Title.
V. Series: Step into reading. Step 4 book.   PZ8.H2944 Han 2004 [E]—dc21   2002152417

Printed in the United States of America   38 37 36 35 34

STEP INTO READING® STEP 4

Hans Christian Andersen's

The Little Mermaid

retold by Deborah Hautzig
illustrated by Darcy May

Random House 🏠 New York

Far away, at the bottom of the sea, lived the Sea King. He lived with his old mother and his six mermaid daughters.

The youngest was the most lovely of all.
Her skin was like a rose. Her eyes were
deep blue. And she had the most beautiful
singing voice on land or sea.

Like all mermaids, the Little Mermaid
had no legs. Her body ended in a fish's tail.

The mermaids had a wonderful life.
All day long they played and sang.

But the Little Mermaid was happiest
when her grandmother told her stories. She
told all about the world of humans above
the sea.

"When you are fifteen, you can swim up
and see it yourself!" the grandmother said.

The Little Mermaid could hardly wait!

At night she stood by her window and gazed up through the water.

She dreamed of seeing the golden sun and purple clouds, the deep green forests and splendid palaces.

At last the Little Mermaid turned
fifteen. Her grandmother gave her a
long string of pearls to wear. The Little
Mermaid kissed her grandmother
good-bye.

"Come back soon," said Grandmother.

"I will!" said the Little Mermaid.

And she swam up through the water,
swift and clear as a bubble.

The Little Mermaid put her head up out of the sea.

In front of her was a big ship. She swam to the window to look inside.

She saw a big party with many people. The handsomest of all was a young prince.

She could not take her eyes off him!

Instantly, there was a loud clap of
thunder. Lightning filled the sky, and the
seas began to rise. A terrible storm raged.
The waves slapped the Prince's ship,
harder and harder—until the great ship
broke apart!

The Little Mermaid saw the Prince fall into the sea.

"The Prince will drown!" she cried. "I must save him!"

The Little Mermaid went diving down to look for him.

The Little Mermaid found the Prince.
She swam up through the water with him.

She held his head above the sea and took
him to shore.

She gently put the Prince on the sand and
kissed his forehead.

Then the mermaid swam and hid
behind a large rock. "I cannot leave until
someone comes to help him," the Little
Mermaid vowed.

Soon a pretty girl came along the beach. She had deep blue eyes.

The Prince woke up and smiled at the girl.

He didn't smile at the Little Mermaid. He did not know that it was the Little Mermaid who had saved his life. He did not know she even existed!

The girl led the Prince away.

The Little Mermaid felt so sad to see him go! She swam back home full of sorrow.

Days and weeks went by, but the Little Mermaid did not feel better. She could only think about the Prince.

She missed him so much!

She found out where he lived. The Prince lived in a wonderful white palace by the sea. Many nights the Little Mermaid swam near the palace.

She swam so close! She could see the Prince looking out his window at the sea. How she longed to be near him once again!

The Little Mermaid loved the world
above the sea more and more.

"Grandmother," she asked one day,
"can people live forever?"

"No," said her grandmother. "People
die, as we do. But when mermaids die, we
become foam on the water. Humans have a
soul that lives forever."

"Could I get a human soul?" asked the Little Mermaid.

Her grandmother said, "Only if a human loved you with all his heart and married you. Then his soul would flow into your body. He would give you a soul and still keep his own."

That night the Little Mermaid could not sleep.

"I must win the Prince's love and marry him!" cried the mermaid. "Then I will have a soul that will live forever. Maybe the Sea Witch can help me!"

The Sea Witch lived in a house made of the bones of drowned sailors. Hundreds of sea snakes filled the garden.

When the witch saw the Little Mermaid, she said, "I know what you want —a pair of human legs. Then you can walk on land and win the love of the Prince."

The mermaid nodded eagerly.

"You will be sorry!" said the witch. "But I will grant your wish. I will make a magic drink for you. You must swim to land and drink it.

"Then your tail will split in two, and you will have human legs. It will hurt terribly when you walk. Are you ready for that?"

"Yes," said the mermaid. "I am!"

"Remember," the witch warned, "once you are human, you can never become a mermaid again.

"And if the Prince marries someone else, you will not get a human soul. You will turn to foam on the sea!"

The mermaid turned very pale. But she said, "I'm ready."

"First, you must pay me," said the Sea Witch. "You have the prettiest voice on earth or sea. You must give your voice to me."

"But what will I have left?" cried the Little Mermaid.

"Your lovely body, your grace, and your deep blue eyes."

"All right," the mermaid said. "Take it!"

Instantly, the mermaid's voice was gone. She could not speak or sing.

The witch gave the Little Mermaid her magic drink.

The mermaid swam to shore. She sat on the steps of the Prince's palace and drank the magic brew.

The next thing she knew, the Little
Mermaid woke up. She had the prettiest
legs on earth. And in front of her stood the
handsome Prince.

"Who are you?" asked the Prince.
"Where do you come from?"

But the Little Mermaid could not speak.
She could only look at the Prince with her
sad blue eyes.

The Prince took the mermaid's hand and led her into his palace.

Every step felt like sharp knives. But the Little Mermaid didn't mind. She was finally with the Prince!

In the palace, thc Little Mermaid had her own room. She had a bed with a velvet canopy. She had a mirror with a gold frame.

The Little Mermaid wore the finest silk dresses. She was the most beautiful girl in the kingdom.

But she could not speak or sing. Her beautiful voice was gone!

The Prince gave many parties.

One night a group of lovely girls sang
for the mermaid, the Prince, and the royal
family.

The Prince clapped his hands in delight.
This made the mermaid so sad!

"I sang more beautifully than anyone,"
she thought. "If only the Prince knew I
gave away my voice to be with him!"

Next the lovely girls danced.

The Little Mermaid rose up on her toes.
She danced as lightly as a bubble. She
looked more lovely with every step.

Everyone was enchanted, the Prince
most of all!

The Little Mermaid danced and
danced, though it hurt her feet terribly.

"You must never leave me," said the
Prince. "Never!"

The mermaid spent all her days with the Prince.

They did everything together. They had picnics on the beach. They went riding on royal horses in the deep green woods.

They climbed up mountains and looked down at the clouds.

The Little Mermaid's feet ached but she didn't care—she was happy to be with the Prince.

And day by day the Prince loved the mermaid more and more.

"You remind me of a young girl with blue eyes who saved my life," said the Prince. "She is the only girl I can ever love."

The Little Mermaid thought, "Oh, how I wish I could tell him it was me! I saved his life!"

She felt so sad, she thought her heart would break.

Then one day, the Prince had news.

"My parents want me to marry the Princess in the next kingdom. I must visit the Princess. But I know I can't love her. She is not like the girl who saved me, as you are!"

He kissed the Little Mermaid.

Then they got on a royal ship and sailed
off to the next kingdom.

At last they arrived and stepped off the ship.

There was the Princess. She had deep blue eyes, just like the Little Mermaid.

"It's you!" cried the Prince. "You rescued me when I was lying on the shore!"

He held his bride in his arms.

The Prince said to the Little Mermaid, "My wish has come true. I found the girl who saved me! I know you will be happy for me, because I know you love me."

The mermaid felt her heart breaking, but she kissed the Prince's hand.

The wedding was grand!

But the Little Mermaid did not hear the wonderful music or see the merry faces around her.

"This is my last night on earth," she said to herself. "Tomorrow I will be foam on the sea. I have lost everything I love."

The Little Mermaid danced for the last time. She moved like an angel, with a smile on her face but sorrow in her heart.

Then everyone went onto the royal ship.

Late that night the mermaid's sisters
rose out of the sea.

"Little sister!" they cried. "The Sea
Witch gave us a knife. You must kill the
Prince. When his blood splashes on you,
your tail will grow back! You can live under
the sea again!"

The Little Mermaid's eyes opened
wide.

Her sisters cried, "You or the Prince
must die. Kill him and come back to us!
Hurry!"

The Little Mermaid tiptoed into the Prince's room.

He was fast asleep with his bride. How happy they looked together!

The Little Mermaid held up the knife and looked at the Prince she loved. Then she turned and threw the knife into the sea.

The waters turned black where the knife fell.

The Little Mermaid jumped into the sea.

But the Little Mermaid didn't turn
to sea foam.

She rose up into the air. All around her
were hundreds of lovely floating children.

"Who are you?" asked the Little
Mermaid.

She had a new voice! It was more
beautiful than any music.

"We are the children of the air," said the others. "Now you are one of us. There are many ways to win a soul. We have souls because of the good deeds we've done.

"You loved the Prince so much that you gave your life for him. Your soul will live forever!"

The Little Mermaid looked down at
the ship one last time. She floated down,
invisible as the wind, and kissed the Prince
and his bride. Then she flew off into
the sky.